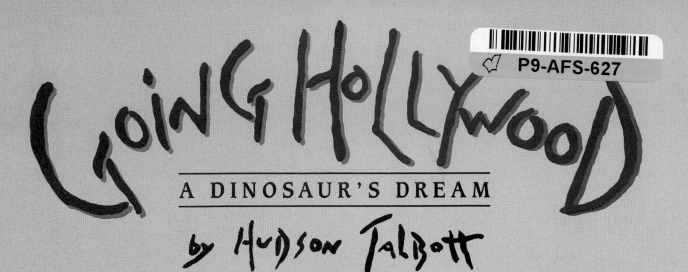

GOING HOLLYWOOD

A DINOSAUR'S DREAM

by Hudson Talbott

Two hundred million years ago,
when dinosaurs ruled the earth,
one mighty reptile was feared most of all.
Me. The tyrannosaurus.
But you can call me Rex.

CROWN PUBLISHERS, INC., NEW YORK

Dragonfly Books

A DRAGONFLY BOOK PUBLISHED BY CROWN PUBLISHERS, INC.

Library of Congress Cataloging-in-Publication Data
Talbott, Hudson.
Going Hollywood: a dinosaur's dream / Hudson Talbott.
Summary: Rex, one of a group of dinosaurs living at the Museum of Natural History, loses his place as the center of attention when a film director invites them all to sunny California.
[1. Dinosaurs–Fiction. 2. California–Fiction.] I. Title.
PZ7.T153Re   1989   89-1190
[E]–dc 19

ISBN 0-517-57354-7 (trade)
0-517-57309-1 (lib. bdg.)
0-517-58983-4 (pbk.)

10 9 8 7 6 5 4 3 2

First Dragonfly Books edition: September 1993

Life has been different ever since we moved
to New York. It all started when a time-traveling
salesman offered seven of us a ride to the
twentieth century. Today we live and work at the
Museum of Natural History with Dr. Miriam
Bleeb. Helping with her lectures was my forte.

"As you see," Dr. Bleeb lectured one day,
"dinosaurian feet were not only excellent for
speed, but also for–"

"Tap dancing!" I blurted.

Unfortunately, I often got carried away.

"Sorry, chief," I stammered. "I-I don't know what came over me. All that *attention*–people *admiring* me instead of running from me–it goes to my head."

"Well, get over it! This is the nineties!" snapped Dr. Bleeb. "Everyone else accepts you for who you are *now* and you better do the same unless you want a one-way ticket back to the Mesozoic era. In any case, there's someone I want you all to meet."

"*Buon giorno, Signori Dinosauri,*" said Dr. Bleeb's guest. "My name is Franco Zeppoli, and I'm making a film about the daily life of dinosaurs. We're using the La Brea tar pits as our location, and I would like you to join us in California–"

"California?!" I interrupted. "As in…

Hollywood!?!" I suddenly realized the possibilities: my name in lights, the adoration of millions, a legend in my own time.

"Now, Rex," countered the chief sharply, "don't go getting ideas. We're going to Hollywood strictly in the name of science. Understand?"

I understood, all right! I had my bags packed and was on our bus within a half hour.

L.A. at last! And it was my turn to drive!

We put the top up to
remain inconspicuous.

We met with Mr. Zeppoli by the tar pits. I was in rare form.

"...and I can do comedy, too!" I was saying. "Listen to this:

"Thank you, but that won't be necessary,"
explained the director. "You see, in this film we're
focusing on the smaller, lesser-known dinosaurs.
I'm calling it *The Life of Dwig*. But I've written
a part for you, too. It's on this napkin."

"*The Life of DWIG?*"
I muttered to myself.
"Who's going to come see *that?*

"I don't get it! How could they pass over *me*– the king of the dinos? The tyrant-lizard? What's Dwig got that I don't have **times ten**?!?!?

" *The Life of Dwig,* eh? Well, I remember what life was like for all those pipsqueaks when I was boss. Why I oughta– I'll show them!"

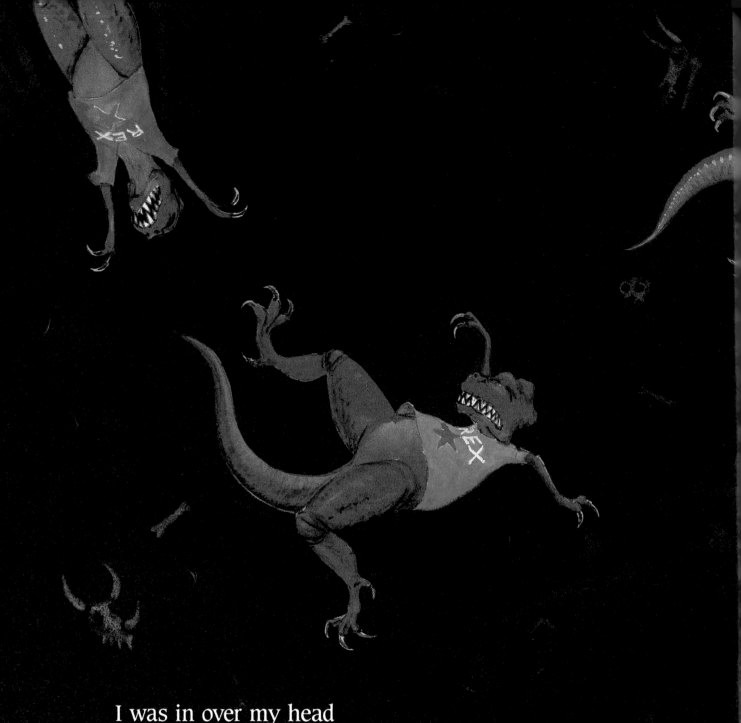

I was in over my head
before I knew what happened.
The more I struggled, the
deeper I sank.

I drifted downward until
I came to a door where a
frighteningly familiar creature
stood.

"Ready for your big scene,
Rex!" he called.

"What big scene?" I asked. "Where am I?"
"This is the final scene of *The Life of Rex*.
You've done a great job of writing and directing
this movie, but I'm afraid your costar steals it
from you. Here he comes now."

"Hey!" I gasped. "Tha-that's *me!*"
What a nightmare! Everywhere I looked I
saw myself staring back at me. This wasn't how
I wanted it to end.

"Hold on there, big fella, I see your point!" I sputtered. "But can we talk this over first? There's something really eating at me!

"I'm sorry for messing things up so much. I don't want to hurt or scare anyone, really I don't, but it's tough being a tyrannosaurus in the twentieth century. And let's face it—I still have a lot to learn! Couldn't we forget this movie stuff and just get to know each other?

"I sure could use a friend."

My gigantic other self looked quizzical
and then cleared his throat. "Well, why not?
We could give it a try!"

Rex . . . . . . Rex . . . . . . Rex . . . . . .

"Rex. Rex?" It was
Dr. Bleeb's voice.
"Are you all right, Rex?"

"Wha...Where am I?" I asked, opening my eyes. "Is this heaven?"

"Not quite, my boy," answered Dr. Bleeb. "But you weren't far from it. We had quite a time pulling you out of that tar pit."

"You mean I'm still here?" I wheezed.
"Listen, guys, I've been acting like a monster lately
and I'm sorry. I really want to learn from my
mistakes. I hope you can forgive me for them."
   "Of course we can, Rex," said Dwig.
"You're our pal, our buddy, our best
friend, and we'd all like to hug you. But
would you mind taking a bath first?"

After dinner, the boys
mapped out their tour of
the stars' homes while I
continued to scrub myself.
It felt good to get clean.